Printed in the United States
By Bookmasters

ASUNDER

OTHELLO LENEER GRAHAM

SPOTLIGHT

Matthew 26:41

(In The Beginning)

Rex and Sloan Davenport are who many would consider as having it all. Both are endowed with 5 worldly excepted/ worshipped, universal values: Physical Attractiveness, Wealth, Influence, Health and being Anglo Saxon! Rex and Sloan possess Doctorates. Sloan is a Dermatologist and Plastic Surgeon. Rex is an Ordained Minister, holding a Doctorate in Theology. Rex is a Theology Professor at the local university; thriving secularly, yet devout Christians. Business is booming in both their respective positions. Their household is also well adjusted; a set of valedictorian twins. Nonetheless, with uncanny, targeted timing, a wicked wind blows. Murphy's Law is about to set up camp in Southern Belle Georgia.

Mallory and Jordy have been raised in a Christian home since birth. They have attended private, Christian schools as a result. It's odd we have to be taught how to be respectful, however; misbehavior is ingrained. "So, what's up Jo-Jo? Are you and Jeremiah gonna do the nasty?" "Mal, I wish you wouldn't say such things. You know I'm trying to live for the Lord, and you should be too," remarks Jordy scolding her twin. "This lifestyle is just so boring. Jeremiah is cool, but he's just a farmhand. All he knows are cows and pigs. I wanna date a hot guy like Heath, he's such a bad boy," remarks Mallory shaking her booty! "Well, that's the difference between us. You're awfully impulsive and vain." The twins continue to walk home from school. Although they are the spitting image of each other, their persona couldn't be more dissimilar. You have "Little House on The Prairie" on one hand, and "The Kardashians" on the other!

The twins arrive at the ranch. The ranch they reside upon has Arabian horses with vast picturesque acreage that would nearly put the "Ponderosa" to shame! The Davenports have the world as their pearl. While Jordy is immersed in her studies, Mallory is engulfed with her social media addictions. Mallory tosses Jordy her homework assignments.

(Blackmailing a Twin)

"Hey Jo-Jo, I need for you to finish up my English Literature assignment. I have a test soon. We are gonna do the 'Switch-eroo' when I have my test." Looking up from her books, Jordy exhales being cross with Mallory. "I don't feel comfortable being deceitful by taking your place during all your tests Mallory. If the school, or Mom and Dad ever found out, we would be grounded for life." Mallory scoffs. "Damn, chill out Jo-Jo, it's not that severe." Mallory has Intel hanging over Jordy. "If you don't wanna cooperate, I can tell the folks about when you got caught trying to smoke a cigarette at school trying to be one of the cool kids." "That was one stupid mistake; a momentary lapse of good judgement. I nearly gagged myself to death. I can't stand cigarettes." Mallory smiles as the cat toying with the mouse. "You know I don't bluff. Mom and Dad expect me, the wild child to act out, but never you snowflake." "Ok, ok. I'll do it," states Jordy with uneasiness.

"Hey girls, I'm home." Sloan announces her presence up the spiral staircase. Moments later, Rex enters as if he was 'Ward Cleaver' from "Leave it to Beaver." It was a busy day for both parents. "Come on down girls, we're having Italian food tonight." The girls didn't respond. "Let me go upstairs to get the girls," replies Rex. "No need, I got this," remarks Sloan. She reaches in her designer handbag for her cellphone. She knows how females are attached to their cellphones; so, she texts them instead. Within seconds, the girls are heading downstairs gathering at the dinner table. Mallory was getting ready to dig in until she was admonished by her Father to say grace. The four hold hands while Rex recites a family dinner prayer. "So, how was school today?" poses Rex and Sloan in unison. In usual manner, Jordy bursts with enthusiasm chronicling her colossal day. "Well Mallory, how about you?" inquires Sloan. Rolling her eyes, Mallory replies… "It's cool Mom. The 'New Math' is a bitch though." "Mallory, please watch your language," responds Rex. Sloan and Jordy just shake their heads.

(This Witch is a Bitch)

It's family game night. "Who's up for some Monopoly, or Twister?" eagerly speaks Rex. "C'mon Pops, we are far too old for this. You behave like the dad from 'Brady Bunch.' This isn't 1971. Get real please." Mallory isn't having any of it. "Well Dad, you know I'm normally on board for game night, however; I'm swamped tonight. I've got to study, and do a surprise English Literature assignment." Jordy sharply looks at her twin with disapproval. Rex looks to Sloan for support. She's empathic but also declines. "I'm sorry sweetie we're all bailing on you. I've got a full booking of clients tomorrow at the practice. Many of them are super vain regarding their facial lines." "I understand honey. I'll just retire to the study to review scriptures for tomorrow's class lecture." Everyone goes their separate ways for the evening.

The following day, all four clan members are like mice in a maze. Sloan is trying to be a miracle worker/ magician with her scalpel. All of her clients are privileged, distinguished, elitist socialites, offenders of the... 'The Hoi Polloi.' Nips, tucks, lifts and collagen are the recipe for VIP vanity. One of Sloan's most difficult clients, Augusta Wilberforce, has had so many procedures; she looks like a clownish, melting, wax figure. Beauty is skin deep, but ugly goes to the bone! In Augusta's case, it's "Trick or Treat" on a daily basis! Due to Sloan's impeccable reputation, and oath to ethics, she empathetically informs Augusta that she can no longer perform additional cosmetic procedures in good conscience. After breaking the sour news to Augusta, Sloan hands Augusta a list of Plastic Surgeon referrals in the area. Augusta replies in snooty huff: "How embarrassing! Apparently, you aren't familiar with my pedigree. I'm a descendant of royal blood my dear! I have connections you wouldn't believe child!" Sloan chuckles ever so slightly. "Judging by your 'Cro-Magnon' bone structure, freckles, splotchy complexion and red hair, probably from decades of incest I'm assuming." Augusta is embarrassed beyond belief! Augusta rises up snatching her Kentucky derby type women's hat then puts on her designer shades. "No one insults Augusta Wilberforce and gets away with it!" Augusta storms out enraged!

(A Southern Belle from Hell)

Rex's day has been unsettling too. During a class Biblical lecture, one of his students debates him tit for tat. Rex maintains his professionalism viewing it as youthful zeal for learning. Still the male needles him as if it was a "Salem Witch Trial." Rex peers over his rimmed glasses. "Damien, please bridle your disrespectful outbursts. I welcome banter; however, you have surpassed civility at this juncture young man." Other students are on the edge of their seats in anticipatory mode! Damien continues to rant with increased coarseness! Removing his glasses, Rex declares… "Damien, you are relieved of your student duties from this class. You are formally dismissed with a grade of "F." Damien rises to his feet then striking the table with his fist declaring… "I am a Wilberforce of royal ancestry. My family has been governing this town since it was founded! You haven't heard the last from me!" Damien exits, slamming the door with fury! Rex takes a moment to compose himself, then gets back to his lesson not missing a beat!

Days are steamy during Georgia Summers. Mallory is up to her normal, fly by the seat of her pants routine. During class change, she sees Heath exiting the gym. Heath is perspiring as a hog narrowly escaping the slaughterhouse!

Mallory takes golden advantage of noticing her quarry. "Hi Heath, looks like you practiced hard today." Out of the blue, a hot-tempered red head appears. "No other females besides teachers are allowed to speak to Heath. He's completely off limits! I'm gonna court him soon. Perhaps you didn't get the memo, or seen my 'Look Book' page, but I'm Scarlett Wilberforce; a descendant of royal blood; the first family settling in this county during colonial times. Consider yourself on notice. Come Heath, let's go." Heath mouths the word 'sorry' to Mallory. The pair walk arm in arm down the corridor to the student union.

(Author's Rant)

Jordy is a teacher's pet in her Honors Calculus class. (Well, she's a teacher's pet in all her courses). Her sole competition on a scholarly basis is Broderick. He's a snippy, entitled, arrogant, nerdy, abrasive, aloof bookworm. He's a borderline grotesque, caricature resembling a ventriloquist's dummy with jutting cheekbones! When the bell rings, Broderick stalks Jordy to her locker. She's startled as she removes books from her bag! "Let me tell you how this is going to go down from now on. "You may think you are all that with your blonde hair and blues eyes, but I'm the 'Alpha Mind' at this school. Tone it down Missy. I'm a Wilberforce with royal heritage; I've got a full scholarship in the balance." After his supposedly intimidating speech, Broderick snaps his fingers while twitching his neck from side to side! Jordy notices Broderick's glittery nail polish. Jordy snickers from his over the top gay display!

It's been a difficult day for the Davenports. Jordy and Mallory head home on foot since they reside so close to the school. On this particular day, Jordy pauses to admire God's Creation. The flora is a visual and olfactory feast! She literally stops to smell the Roses. "These flowers are so stunning aren't they Mallory?" Mallory sighs, and then twirls her golden hair. "Yea, they are ok. I'd rather be admiring Heath McPherson's Adonis type body. He's so rugged and chiseled." Mallory is miffed at her twins' dismissive posture. "Mal, why don't you get your head out of the clouds? You are missing what's right in front of you." Mallory pops her chewing gum while posting selfies on her "Look Book" page. After a few more moments of absorbing the green ambiance, Jordy begins to walk off. She has to literally snatch Mal from chatting so hard online. Mallory's face remains buried in her cellphone. **(Author's Rant: What's up with the mind numbing social media addiction associated with millennials? Some probably can't even take a dump without texting, or being logged in! Careful, don't fumble your phone while wiping your booty! Moreover, stop texting and taking selfies while driving! It's not that important! It is reckless though, duh!)**

(An Unlikely Visitor)

Rex is quite the home cook. He enjoys preparing dinner when he can. This evening, he makes Sloppy Joes, coleslaw, salad and baked beans. Rex's iced tea is his own exclusive; so much so, when he makes it he ensures he's in the kitchen alone. His family doesn't even know the ingredients! The girls are upstairs. Sloan gets home later due to the delicacy of cosmetic procedures. "Oh my Lord, Rex; are you preparing Sloppy Joes and tea?" Rex turns around with his perfectly jawed/symmetrical smile, appearing adorable in his apron. "Yes dear. It's been a monstrous day. I thought the family would enjoy." Sloan places her French purse on the kitchen island. Due to Rex's towering height advantage, she stands on tip toes to smooch her man.

Warm spices and seasonings slowly meander upstairs. Seconds later, the girls shout with glee... "It's Sloppy Joe night!" Even the super cool Mallory loses her indifference. They bum rush downstairs as children on their first Christmas Day. Sloan sets the table with Martha Stewart elegance even though it's just Sloppy Joes! The family joins hands to pray. It's Mallory's turn. With heads bowed and eyes closed (so it appears), prayer commences. Hearing fingernail taps next to her, Jordy opens her eyes. Mallory is

11

texting while praying! As a result, Jordy pinches her twin in correction. Mallory resumes the prayer properly. "Let's dig in everybody," speaks Sloan passing platters around.

"Ding-Dong; The door bells rings." Mallory opts to answer the door so she could snap more selfies. She was too enthralled with her egotistical whims to ask who was at the front door before opening it. "Hello." It's Heath McPherson. Mallory drops her phone on the plush carpeting in shock. "Who is it Mallory?" poses Rex heading towards Mallory. Still in awe, Mallory stutters. "It's, it's Heath from school. Rex gives Heath a firm handshake. Wondering what's taking so long, Sloan accompanies Jordy to the door.

(Kitchen Cunnilingus)

"Well, invite the young man in Mallory," says Rex after the introductions were done. "Thanks so much Sir, but I'm on a delivery. I wanted to bring Mallory some fresh cupcakes from my job as a peace offering. I work part-time at Paradise Pastries. Mallory was given the cold shoulder today at school by a 'not so nice' person. I have secret aspirations of becoming an executive Pastry Chef one day. If kids at school found out, I would never live it down." Heath hands the gooey, frosted delights to Mallory. She blushes. "Well, goodnight everyone," replies Heath as he hurries to his 1990's 4X4. Mallory closes the door as the gang heads back to the kitchen. "He seems to be a nice boy, and kind of cute too," comments Sloan with a grin. Jordy nods in accordance. "Yea, I gotta admit Mal; he's not the run-of-the-mill Valdosta jock. He would be a great influence on you." Rex chimes. "I agree. He has a boy scout type charm." As they settle back in to eat, the quad shares the experiences of their day. As each recalls, an ironic common denominator surfaces. It's uncanny how the name 'Wilberforce' shadows them. Consequently, Rex is led to pray. "Everyone join hands. Lord, please keep your hedge around us; not permitting the enemy to kill, steal or destroy."

"Amen." Afterwards, Mallory opens the box of cupcakes. To her astonishment, there was a card taped inside the lid. "I baked these myself Mallory. I hope everyone enjoys." "Mmmmm, these are so delicious!" Sloan rejoices while licking the gooey chocolate peanut butter crème from her lips. It's a consensus. The cupcakes are a homerun! Nice pun since Heath is a High School All-American Baseball player! The twins excuse themselves; Jordy more so. "Mom and Dad, we have an English Literary assignment to do." Mallory grins on the sneak tip.

After the twins fall asleep, Rex and Sloan slip to the kitchen gorging their sweet tooth. Rex Finger paints peanut butter crème on Sloan's toes and soles! She giggles heavily. He orally vacuums both her feet. His tongue darts like a serpent's. Rex finishes her off with kitchen cunnilingus! That's how it's done!

(The claws come out)

Tit for tat, make this like that. It's time for Jordy to switch places with her twin for Mallory's test. Jordy has mimicked the role well. She dresses scantily ensuring her parents never witness the transformation trickery. Mallory applies Jordy's make-up as the final touch. She resembles a washed up 80's pop star. Jordy's metamorphosis is stellar assuming her twins' persona. It's as if she has an alter ego awakening; A Jekyll and Hyde mode. Although Jordy has been keeping her sister afloat academically with impersonation, this time it feels different... intoxicatingly alluring. It's full frontal. Jordy goofs around during testing appearing to be perplexed although she isn't. She procrastinates playing with her hair. The teacher announces how much time is remaining. Jordy paces herself answering questions. She intentionally answers several incorrectly. She knows Mallory never earns a perfect score. After class dismisses, she goes to Mallory's locker for book exchange. Heath McPherson stops to say Hi. "Hi Mallory, I hope you and your family liked the cupcakes I made." Jordy mentally composes her reply. "They were to die for Heath. I even snapped some pics." "I'm glad you all enjoyed them, but please keep that between us. As I mentioned last night, I don't want everyone to know I like baking. Well, I gotta head to class; chat with you later." As Heath departs, Jordy becomes smitten.

The school bell rings. The girls catch up on the latest while walking home. "So, how did things go with testing Jo-Jo? Did you pull it off?" "Yes, everything went according to plan. Although I knew all the answers, I missed a few on purpose to make it look good. If you made a 100, she would have known something was up." Mallory fist bumps Jordy. "Way to go Jo-Jo. As long as you play ball, I will never tell the peeps about you trying to cop a smoke." "Geez Mal, it was one pull and I nearly hocked a lung." "I'm cool if you are. I won't tell if you don't." Mallory rolls her eyes in displeasure. "You sound like a Republican in office right now!" Jordy walks faster trying to outpace her sister in anger. Jordy mentally recalls her Heath encounter. Two can play this game she ponders.

(4.0 GPA — The Fragrance)

The following day, Rex and Sloan meet for a lunch date at the acclaimed 'Surf and Turf' Tower. Routine gender roles are reversed. Rex opts for seafood, while Sloan craves a big ole ribeye! As the marital duo chat, familiar voices trickle in the VIP dining area. Both Rex and Sloan turn around to fulfill their curiosity. They see what appear to be two fiery, red headed individuals. As they become visible, it's Augusta and Damien Wilberforce. Augusta had her children later in life, Broderick, Scarlett and Damien. She presents as a grandparent in her elderly appearance. As they pass Rex and Sloan, the four make eye contact. A figurative chill is cast from the red haired snobs. Sensing something's afoot, Rex immediately clutches his wife's hand. He murmurs a silent prayer. The Wilberforce's glance their direction with piercing intent. The Davenport's savor the individual flavors of ocean, and bovine over a glass of wine. The server inquires if they want dessert. They pause then smile recalling their cupcake escapades! Sloan replies… "We'll politely decline. We have some cupcakes at home we gonna polish off tonight." Rex blushes profusely from his wife's innuendo! The Wilberforce's scour in their direction. Moments later, Rex and Sloan depart heading back to work.

Later that afternoon, a new patient sits in Dr. Sloan's waiting room. Her receptionist summons him to Sloan's exam room for a consultation. Sloan is quite flabbergasted! Her eyes glaze as a deer in headlights. "It's you. You're the young man who bought us cupcakes. What in the world brings you to my office?" Sloan glances embarrassingly at Heath's paperwork trying to recall his name. "Please have a seat Mr. McPherson." "Please, call me Heath Ma'am." Heath is very courteous, and damn easy on the eyes. "Well Dr. Davenport, as you can see, my face is breaking out. Acne bumps are hitting homeruns while I strike out. Sloan did recall Heath played baseball. She examines his face with tactile accuracy. Her fingertips provide a gentle comfort during facial exploration. Her hands examine as well as caress. As she probes further, Sloan asks Heath an unrelated question. "What's the name of the cologne you're wearing?" Heath lowers his head with a rosy blush. "It's called 4.0 GPA". Sloan takes another aromatic whiff. She drops her pen with aromatic intoxication!

(More Peanut Butter Passion)

Being chivalrous, Heath stoops over retrieving Sloan's pen. "Here you are Ma'am." Sloan is now flushed with blush! She clears her throat to resume for Hippocratic duties. Sloan prescribes a facial wash, and topical ointments to manage Heath's acne. She also gives him free samples. "Please follow the regimen. You will see fantastic results after 3 weeks. I'm scheduling a follow up in 30 days." She catches another contact high from Heath's 4.0 GPA cologne. "Ummm, I'm gonna waive my charge for your next visit. Of course Heath it goes without saying, that's our little secret." "Thank you so much Ma'am!" He follows up with a hug. Heath's visit was the highpoint of Sloan's day. After work, Sloan darts uptown to Jean's Department Store. An eager, commissioned teen greets her. "How can I assist?" Sloan appears frantic. "Please tell me you have a men's fragrance called 4.0 GPA." Missy replies… "It's been our hottest seller. Let me check our counter stock." Sloan fidgets as if waiting on pregnancy test results! Missy returns with a green and gold tinted box. "Yes Ma'am. This is our last box. It's been selling so well people have even begged to buy our tester bottle." Sloan is ecstatic!

Rex decides to prepare an ethnic family dish. Tonight's

menu is Curry Chicken with spiced veggies. He adds a bit of whimsy by wearing a chef's hat he purchased at a Farmer's Market after work. It's a laugh riot! Even 'Millennial Mallory' is in stiches! After everyone composes themselves, Sloan was eager to share her news of Heath coming to her office. However, she rapidly recants her Hippocratic Oath of patient confidentiality. Attention soon shifts to the remaining cupcakes Heath supplied; only 3 remain. Once the twins make their upstairs retreat, Rex nabs the 3 cupcakes. Sloan reaches in her purse retrieving the fragrance. "Put this on." Rex obeys. Keeping with the prior escapades, Rex removes Sloan's sexy heels. Sloan assumes the position. He again lathers the peanut butter cream frosting generously upon Sloan's shapely, arched soles. Passion ensues. Bodily fluids are reciprocated.

(White Females Love Bagels)

After catching their breaths, Sloan's keen female olfactory system makes a discovery. The cologne doesn't exude the same erotic chemistry upon Rex as it does on Heath. She is disillusioned. After showering, the pair disinfects the linoleum and kitchen. Finding themselves exhausted, they quickly drift off majestically on their King Size, Mahogany Bed.

The following morning rolls around. The couple awakens. Rex begins to caress his wife's hair. "Sweetheart, thank you for last night; it was terrific. However, the cologne smelled ok, but it didn't appeal to me. It was too adolescent. Perhaps you could donate it to a worthy cause like a thrift store, or something. I know since it's been opened, it can't be returned or exchanged. I love you babe for the thought nonetheless." "Last night was wonderful Rex. You are right, identical scents can vary from person to person. I'm not upset dear. As a matter of fact, I will do as you suggested. I'll donate the cologne to a worthy cause." The two kiss then prepare for work. Mallory is craving a cupcake with breakfast. She opens the fridge eyeballing its contents. "Like, WTF? Jo-Jo you are such a pig eating all the leftover cupcakes!" Jordy looks up to Mallory away from her cream cheese bagel. "So not true Mal." Rex and Sloan stare at each other with embarrassment. "Your Mom and I liquidated… I meant ate the remaining cupcakes last night." Rex catches himself. "Pops, you and Mom are so busted right now." Jordy just shakes her head in disbelief. "Just grab a bagel instead Mal and grow up. They are gluten free." After consuming their bagels, the twins snatch their book bags about to head out. "Oh, by the way Mallory, what does WTF mean?" "Really Rex? You don't know?" poses Sloan. Sloan leans whispering in her hubby's ear. Rex is appalled! "Such language Mallory." Jordy snickers. "Now who's busted?"

As the day unfolds, Rex grades a few term papers during his office hours. He sips his thermos full of his homemade iced tea. Rex's door is ajar. A visitor taps lightly on his door. "Please come in." "Good Afternoon Dr. Davenport." "Is that you Heath?" "Yes Sir." Rex embraces Heath with a hug. "What brings you to my office young man?" Heath removes his baseball cap to address Rex.

(The Stench of Sexiness)

"Well Sir, I wanted to speak to you about a matter. As I mentioned to you when I delivered the cupcakes, I'm gonna major in Culinary Arts. I love baking. My desire is to become a Pastry pioneer. I want to minor in Religious Studies. I hear you are the best Professor in the field. I'm hoping to be one of your students after High School Graduation." Rex is moved by Heath's sentiments. Rex ponders rubbing his chin. "Tell you what I'm willing to do. I'm willing to tutor you no charge after school between your job and baseball practice. We'll keep this between you and I. Heath is overjoyed! "By the way Heath, what's the name of the cologne you're wearing? My wife would love it." "It's called '4.0 GPA' Sir. See you later." Rex is amazed how much better the cologne smells on Heath versus himself!

Weeks pass. While impersonating Mallory during tests, Jordy's personality morphs. She becomes edgier; more intense. Her parents are oblivious though as many are. Jordy is able to mimic a chameleon. Mallory isn't so thrilled. She likes being the Alpha Female between the two. "Jeremiah asked about you today Jordy. He's shy with awkwardness. He seems genuine. I may have been wrong about him. At first, he thought I was you from a distance." Jordy rolls her eyes dismissively. "You were right in the beginning Mal. Jeremiah is basic and safe. My tastes have broadened my dear, younger sister." Mallory reacts. "Younger? You're only like 3 minutes older than me." "Checkmate, I rest my case," Jordy remarks.

Due to baseball practice, Heath arrives late for his follow-up appointment with Sloan. He didn't have sufficient time to shower and change. He's drenched in perspiration, and his clothes are soiled in grass stains. He radiates primal essence. Fortunately, the lobby has emptied. Sloan's receptionist is highly efficient, yet can be aloof. She communicates Dr. Davenport is ready to see him. Instead of escorting him this occasion, she says… "You know the way." Since office hours have just elapsed, Sloan politely dismisses her receptionist for the day. Heath's athletic, raw state exhilarates his Dermatologist. Sloan gloves up to examine Heath's medical progress.

(Batter Up)

"I'm so sorry and embarrassed Dr. Davenport regarding my appearance and smell." He lowers his head. Sloan smiles to reassure. "I grew up with 3 brothers Heath. Believe me; you are far less offensive than they." Sloan places her index finger under Heath's chin to coax his head back up. Sloan has a delicate touch. Her tactile sensitivity is acute. She incorporates a penlight flashlight to augment visibility. "Heath, the meds appears to be working well. Do me a favor and remove your jersey so I can examine your shoulders and back. Sometimes flare ups can spread to various areas of the body." After removing his shirt, Sloan receives a familiar contact high. Heath does as instructed then lies on his stomach. His musculature is well established. "Um, are you wearing that 4.0 GPA Cologne Heath?" "Yes Ma'am. I hope it's not funky along with my perspiration." Actually, the macho pheromones of sweat, oils and fragrance lit Sloan's clit! "Stand up Heath. Please lower your pants and underwear. I just wanna be extra thorough." "Are you serious?" "Underwear for acne?" Sloan develops a shimmer in her eyes.

Heath unlaces his cleats to remove them, and peels off his athletic socks. He then lowers his pants exposing boxers with jock strap equipped with cup. Sloan is being killed softly! Not being able to hold her philly in the stable, she unfastens Heath's jock strap. Sloan is in a stupor! This beefy jock has a skyscraper cock! Sloan reaches in her purse handing him a bottle of 4.0 GPA Cologne. "Please put more of this on! It drives me crazy!" Heath spritzes himself in all the right places. Sloan gawks at his manhood while quickly ripping off her clothing! "Time for you to slide your baseball bat into my centerfield." It takes two hands, and damn near a crane to hoist his wooden pole. Once inside, his veiny girth slides into first, second, third and fourth bases. He glides effortlessly in Sloan's dugout. Sloan is panting as her loins scream. Showers are in the forecast! Heath floods his thick monsoon as Sloan simultaneously sprinkles her diamond! It's a shut out." After a few minutes of afterglow, Sloan grabs her cellphone pulling up her calendar. "Let's schedule another follow-up appointment to make sure all the kinks regarding your regimen are worked out. "Sounds like a plan. Let's do it," states Heath. "Oh, by the way, bring some peanut butter cream cupcakes."

(Sly Sloan)

"Hey Jo-Jo, I'm thinking about finally asking Heath on a date, but I have to be careful. That bitch at school who threatened to make my life hell if I ever got caught near Heath again." "Yea, I remember when we talked about our encounters over dinner a while back. My nemesis threatened to do irreparable damage if I didn't mellow out by dumbing down in class." "You know Mal, he's not worth it. You know those types; he'll pop you then drop you. That's how athletes operate. You don't want that do you Mal? Besides, that's not God's plan." "No, but he's just so hot," replies Mallory smacking her gum. The pair resumes their individual pursuits upstairs.

Rex is downstairs in his study reviewing Bible Scriptures for tomorrow's Theology lecture. "I'm home guys! It's Greek tonight! I got pitas and gyros." Sloan announces to her brood. Soon she is greeting by the clan at the table. As she sets the table, Rex observes Sloan's disheveled demeanor. "Hey Sweetie? Are you Ok? You look like you've been through a war zone." "Yea Mom, what gives?" inquires Jordy. "It was a frontal assault, I was pounded today." Sloan grimaced after her faux pas; hoping no one caught on. "I'm so sorry sweetie." Rex wraps his arms around his wife. "Is that a new perfume, or detergent you are using sweetie?" Sloan is sly. "It was probably contact with a patient I brushed against by accident." "Alright peeps, enough yammering, let's eat." Mallory is eager to dig in. "Not before we have grace lady Mallory," interjects Rex. Having a flashing guilt trip, Sloan says grace. She wants to ask God's forgiveness, but it would be for naught. The Davenport's relish their Greek dinner over small talk.

The next day, Heath shoots Rex a text about tutoring after school. It takes Rex a few hours to respond due to teaching. However, Rex gives the go ahead to arrive around 6pm at his office. After breaking the ice with some baseball banter, Rex gives Heath an introduction to Religious Studies/Theology. Heath is enthused. "I'm happy you want to minor in Religious Studies Heath. I'm confident you will be a great student."

(Sliding Into Home Base)

Heath moves in closer to view Rex's computer screen. After he inches closer, Rex is stricken. He becomes a slave to a repressed, sexual desire he's fantasized about. Rex begins to massage Heath's leg. He gazes into Heath's eyes expressing a dormant passion without uttering a word. Heath is coaxed into passion as he guides Rex's hand. Rex closes his laptop. He rises to his feet in anticipation; Heath does likewise. As if he was trying to maintain a shred of decency, Rex does not undress himself. Instead, he instructs Heath to do the honors. Heath then proceeds to reveal his birthday suit. Rex is awestruck by the vision! "You are packing a Louisville Slugger for real! I'm so embarrassed by my man meat in comparison to you." "Don't be Sir." Heath gets on all fours atop Rex's cloth futon. With muscled buttocks in his sights, Rex makes entry. Heath intentionally clinches and releases stimulating Rex's manhood. Rex realizes his cock has never been this excited. He also realizes what he's doing is spiritually condemning, but he just can't resist his lust induced urges! "You must be wearing that 4.0 GPA Cologne. It smells so sexy on you! Heath replies, "Yes Sir," while he was being banged. Moments later, Rex bursts a nut the size of a fried egg inside Heath's anal cavity. Heath is not far behind pumping his jack spewing pearlescent man milk like paint splattered museum art work! "That was a great first start Heath. We'll have to brush up again soon. Please bring some peanut butter cream cupcakes next time so I can orally polish the cream from your bat." Heath smiles gingerly. The pair dresses. Heath heads out first, then Rex several minutes later to distance himself.

Rex is the last to arrive home. "Hey gang, I'm home!" Rex is laden with Japanese take-out in hand. Sloan rushes to his aid. "Hey sweetie, I'm sorry I'm late. I got hung up with a student I was tutoring. We really slammed ourselves in our work." Rex winced. He nearly 'fouled' up verbally. "Are the girls upstairs Sloan?" "Yes babe. Jordy is helping Mallory cram for a quiz tomorrow." "Call them down while I set up the dinner table."

(Horse Whipped)

"This Hibachi Chicken is so delicious. I love that restaurant," Sloan remarks dipping her eggroll in tangy sauce. "Hard day at the rock pile Dad?" "Yea, it was brutal Jordy. He posed a hard situation, but I got him in the end." Freudian slip by Rex, but no one seems to catch the drift. After stuffing themselves, the foursome watches some family programming briefly before retiring upstairs. Rex was so exhausted from "work," he didn't take a shower after undressing. Sloan is by his side. "Hey babe, what's that smell, is that some new cologne?" Rex thinks fast. "No, you know I'm old school babe, that's why I gave you back that 4.0 GPA cologne. It must have been when I grazed a passing student in the corridor. You know how contacts can be." Sloan flashes to her sexual satisfaction with Heath. "Yea, you are right about that babe," remarks Sloan twirling her hair.

The following school day, Heath is approached. It was carefully orchestrated as not to be seen. "Hey Mallory, what's up?" "I've been attracted to you for a while trying not to be obvious, but I can't stop thinking about you." She is flattered. "Would you stop by around 11pm? Everyone is snoring at that time. Just text me before you arrive. I'll meet you in the stable out back." "Ok Mallory, I'll see you tonight." Later that night, Heath arrives promptly. He opens the stable door treading lightly inside. He sees his admirer standing next to a horse. While referring to the male horse's genitals, she asks a question. "Do you have anything crafted like this Heath?" "That's for me to show, and you to know." Heath is led to a fresh bed of hay in the stable loft remotely in the back. Heath shoots erect viewing naked Aphrodite in Georgia! So much so, his faucet drips. He undresses as quicksilver. "Damn Heath, you are a horse on two legs! I want all of it!" Another batting session for Heath! Heath pops that virgin cherry orally, vaginally and anally! There was so much moaning and groaning, the horses began to whinny! "Oh Heath, your cologne is making me insane!" "It's called 4.0 GPA," grunts Heath with a passionate, facial distortion. Tears of ecstasy stream from the buxom babe. Juices squirt in all directions as a freshly squeezed orange! "You are the best cupcake I ever had," states Heath. "Speaking of which, bring some next time for our appetizer my baseball stallion." "Agreed, I'll pitch, you catch."

(Mallory's Mischief)

Over the next several weeks, Heath pummels Team Davenport. He grand slams every time he's up to bat! His cupcakes serve as appetizers, while he is main entrée, and dessert! No one is the wiser he is literally playing the field! Jordy and Mallory take their usual walk home after school. "Hey Jo-Jo, tell Mom and Pops I'll be home a little later. I'm going to the library for a bit." Jordy is astonished! "Wow, you going to the library? Are they giving away iPhones, free Lattes, Kardashian lessons, or who can say the word "like" the most in a sentence, or something else that white girls like you love?" "Like shut up," responds Mallory as she breaks towards the library. Jordy heads on home. Several minutes later, Mallory arrives at her destination, but it's not the library. Instead, it's the sweet shop where Heath works. She hoping he's working. She spots him in her peripheral vision taking out the trash. She quickly runs up asking if he would stop by her house later that evening around 11pm. She instructs him to rendezvous at the barn. She will be waiting for him there. "Sure Mallory," Heath replies with an impish smile. Mallory heads back home as to not alarm her folks being out too long.

The crew is home. Rex is playing 'Chef Boyardee.' He

makes certain no one is around while he combines his famous iced tea. The family has been eating a lot of take-out lately, so he decides to cook in. Since Mallory is the last one to arrive, she gets the honors of setting the table. "So Mal, how did things go at the library? Did you score free passes for unlimited Mochas with soy shots? "Like, Ha, Ha again Jo-Jo. I will score highly though real soon." Rex and Sloan appear befuddled. "Are we missing something here?" questions Rex. "No, Jo-jo just likes to be a smart butt joking I act too much like a stereotypical white girl." "Yea, next she'll be styling her hair up in a bun all the time, driving a Subaru, demanding 'gluten free' foods, and snapping more 'selfies' all over the place while giggling at everything that's not even remotely funny." "We're proud of you Mallory for taking your studies so seriously," replies Sloan. Jordy is fuming mentally since she impersonates Mallory taking her test at times. "No sweat folks, I got it all under control." The family dines on a home cooked meal before later meandering upstairs.

(Deception Revelation)

An hour before midnight, Heath shows up at the Davenport's barn. Mallory escorts him by the hand to the upstairs loft. She has a fresh bed of hay stacked neatly. "Heath, you smell so sexy." Heath leans in closer to give Mallory a deeper whiff of his scent. "I get so many compliments on it. 4.0 GPA cologne is the best I ever owned." Heath's essence shrouds her. She strips down to her birthday suit. Heath removes his tank top and athletic shorts. Mallory is drooling. "Sock it to me Heath! Ram me as you do homeruns!" He swings his wood as a major leaguer should! Mallory arches her body with synchronized shivers during every sweet stroke. "Ohhhhhhhh, I gonna cum!" bellows Mallory with immense intensity. Heath follows as if he was Tarzan! Mallory is winded. Her body glistens as morning dew upon green grass. Heath sticks out his chest in conquest.

"Give me a second Mallory to run to my truck to get the cupcakes I promised you." Mallory is puzzled. "What are you talking about Heath?" "Did you forget Mallory? You asked me to bring cupcakes the last time we made love." "Made love? Are you high on something right now? I was a virgin up until you!" Mallory festers in a pool of numbness perplexed. Heath only stares. Bit by bit it comes to her. Mallory screams… "JORDY!!!!!!!!!" The horses are so spooked with the shrill; they stampede out of the barn, and over the fencing! Heath quickly dresses hightailing to his truck fearing Mallory's shattered state of mind! Her family is oblivious to what just happened. Full bellies have lulled them into abyss. Mallory remains in the loft sobbing herself into mania.

(Mallory's Mental Madness)

Saturday morning brings much. Mallory is blinded with furious betrayal. She trembles from the loft naked, snatching a pitchfork before she exits! She resembles "Carrie" drenched in perspiration instead of blood! All form of reason has vacated her vessel. She creeps upstairs into her shared bedroom. Jordy is laid across her bed soundly. Suddenly, her cellphone vibrates awakening her. "You slept with my Heath!" Mallory is peering over her poised to impale! "You slept with Heath you treacherous bitch!" "You dressed like me to fool Heath into sleeping with you! Jordy screams and shrieks! Both twins are trembling with nausea and terror! Hearing the commotion, Rex leaps out of bed dashing to aid Jordy. Sloan is right behind him. Rex and Sloan are shocked beyond comprehension witnessing their daughter nude with pitchfork in hand! Rex begins to pray while Sloan pleads with her offspring. "Mallory, please snap out of it! We all love you!" "Love? This bitch impersonated me to smash the boy I liked! He was banging me while he thought of you! You call that love!" Instantly, vivid flashbacks of sexual periods with Heath haunt the minds of Rex and Sloan simultaneously! All four of them experienced sex with Heath!

The couple is able to talk Mallory down from nearly murdering her sister. The four remain in the room motionless gripped mentally in their personal purgatory. Minutes elapse when strangers enter their home marching upstairs. Mallory mistakenly left the front door ajar when she initially came in. The interlopers stood united in the presence of the Davenports. Augusta, Scarlett, Broderick, Damien and Heath are present! "Remember me Dr. Sloan? You insulted me a while back in your office stating I was unfit for additional plastic surgery." Sloan is numb. Mallory, Jordy and Rex also are also sickened by the gathering; their hearts pound. "Broderick, Damien and Scarlett are my children; Heath is my **"Nephew."**

(Mark 10:9)

"I demanded he infiltrate your entire family. He told me in graphic detail how much each of you loved having sex with him. Rex exploring his repressed homosexual curiosity, Sloan living on the wild side, and twins having their virginity stripped away," divulged Augusta arrogantly. Heath knew the entire time he was screwing both you girls Mallory and Jordy although you are twins. Jordy's eyes are much bluer." All the Davenport's dirty linen had been exposed! Each were blindingly infuriated with each other; but couldn't articulate an utterance due to committing similar sins. Speaking persnickety… "As I warned you before slutty Sloan, no one messes with a Wilberforce, and gets away with it." "Y'all got played by the baseball player and struck out. Y'all got had badly!" Heath places an ornate, gift wrapped box on the twins' bedroom floor. Feeling vindicated, the trespassers head downstairs exiting the Davenport home.

After the stupor of sullen silence, Rex stoops over picking up the box. He opens it revealing the contents to his family. It was 4 peanut butter cream cupcakes, and the bottle of 4.0 GPA cologne in which Sloan had given him.

Due to their humiliation, The Davenports relocated to parts unknown trying to mend their broken lives.

"What therefore God has joined together, let no man put asunder."

MEN ARE
Dangerous
(DOGS)

WOMEN ARE
Devious
(SPIDERS)

OTHELLO LENEER GRAHAM

authorHOUSE®

AuthorHouse™
1663 Liberty Drive
Bloomington, IN 47403
www.authorhouse.com
Phone: 833-262-8899

Published by AuthorHouse 12/23/2020

ISBN: 978-1-6655-0289-4 (sc)
ISBN: 978-1-6655-0288-7 (e)

Library of Congress Control Number: 2020919657

King James Version (KJV)
Public Domain

Glimpse. . .

"Dog Bites and Spider Bites Can Kill You!"

(It's a Beautiful Day in The Neighborhood)

"Hey, baby. I'm heading to the gym to hit the weights. I'll text you once I arrive," remarks Hunter. (Hunter is a State Highway Trooper, filling in as Professional Bouncer on some weekends). "Ok sweetie." I'm gonna prune in the garden until you return my love. Sybil blows Hunter a kiss. Hunter reciprocates. Once arriving at the gym, Hunter 'high fives' a few of his buds grinding away at the benches. About 15 minutes into his workout regimen, Hunter notices some guys huddled around the entrance to the Aerobics class. "Normally, these dudes don't ever take a break. I wonder what the commotion is about?" thinks Hunter. Intrigued by the stir, Hunter walks over to investigate the matter. They are eyeing the new Aerobics instructor Dixie aka, "Pageant" due to the countless pageants she has won over her lifetime! (Hunter is no slouch himself. He too is accustomed to the spotlight due to numerous bodybuilding, championship trophies). Rival pageant contestants would often bow out of competitions to save face once they discovered Dixie was in the running! Dixie is so damn hot, it has been said she has converted gay men into straight.

The hunks abandon their workouts after ingesting the celestial body! As if their mainframes had been infiltrated, the huddle head in the locker room to blow off some steam! Each man wanders into a showering stall taking abnormally long showers. Subdued grunts, groans and moaning echo the locker room chamber. They are all masturbating over Dixie! Sadly, Newlywed Hunter shoots the biggest load!

(Sybil, Sybil quite contrary. How does your garden grow)?

Sybil, a young, plain Jane Librarian resembling "Velma" from Scooby Doo, tends her garden as Hunter chisels his sinew. She is also an online Chemistry Student. She loses her virginity to Hunter on their 2nd date. Hunter's football build lures Sybil within his loins. She defines the term "wallflower." Hunter couldn't resist walking down the aisle due to how hard she panted, and her vagina clinching his penis! Busting her cherry was the epitome of icing on a cake! Sybil has been chasing a "Blue Ribbon" for her prized veggies and flora since relocating to Texas from North Dakota where she betroths Hunter. Although she hasn't yet entered any gardening contests, she hears about a woman named "Pageant" who wins every year!

Hunter jogs home from a very brief workout. He notices a Doberman Pinscher, running loose around the city sidewalk. Without provocation, the dog charges at Hunter! Being as big as he his, Hunter was unable to out maneuver the dog. Instead, the dog nips his calf, slightly breaking the skin. Sybil hears him run up. She's like a High School, acne prone, school girl crushing on her male P.E. Teacher!

She swings the wooden back door so hard nearly off its hinges. She jumps into his arms embracing him lovingly. Hunter carries her across the threshold again as they enter the front door. Working in the garden has an aphrodisiac effect on Sybil. Digging in the soil, getting dirt between her fingernails puts her in the mood. She lulls Hunter onto the living room carpeting. She straddles him like a guitar case, riding his banana like a natural born freak! Hunter's foreskin is becoming raw, but it's a small consolation due to his second nut busted within a few hours! He pulls out just in time to scribble/squirt an "H" with his cream on Sybil's ticklish belly! Hunter etches his branding, just like **"Zoro!"** She smears his jizz on her tummy like lotion. After their impromptu bout of sexual frivolity, Sybil wants to make small talk.

(Carpet Conversation)

Twirling Hunter's curly locks, Sybil casually asks, "How was your workout Sweetie? You didn't stay as long as you normally do. Did you pull a muscle, or something?" Hunter grins as recalls "choking his chicken" at the gym. "Yea, um, you can say that." Wanting to be attentive to her man, Sybil offers to get some ice for his injury. Hunter quickly replies… "That won't be necessary baby. I've already *massaged* it."

(Bitten and Smitten by Fate)

The following day, Hunter and Sybil decide to play hooky from work; each phoning in ill to pursue their independent passions. Sybil is being proactive, staying ahead of her online chemistry coursework. Afterwards, she makes a light snack, tuna on wheat, for her and a well done, yet juicy Angus beef burger for Hunter. As a bodybuilder, Hunter craves his meat protein! At the table, they gaze into each other's eyes as lost sheep. Hunter informs Sybil he will be at the gym the majority of the day. Lucky for him, no one from work came in! Sybil mentions she will toil in her garden trying to nurture prize winning veggies and flowers. The two part ways with a loving peck on the cheeks.

While adding fertilizer to her lilies, she accidently disturbs the web of a robust, garden spider. "Ouch!" speaks Sybil as she quickly swipes the spider off. She sees two minor puncture wounds, but continues to garden. She is not worried because she is up to date with her tetanus shots. A few minutes later, she feels a bit lightheaded. A downstairs nap soon follows.

Hunter and his gym buddies work up a major sweat. Each glistens as morning dew upon grass. They spot one another as gym code. Hunter becomes the ring leader, as

he is the most muscular. While exuding machoism, Hunter herds the group towards Dixie's aerobics class. Once again they ogle at her perfectly dimensioned bouncing boobs! It's like watching a perpetual tennis match! "Soon, I'm gonna tap that ass", Hunter brags while flexing his pecs, biceps and triceps. "We know you are married the group whispers to him. We see the tan line on your ring finger stud. We all remove our wedding rings prior to coming to the gym! Oldest trick in the playbook. Busted dude!" They chuckle amongst themselves. After getting an eye full of Dixie, their nether regions in the "South Pole" engorge with blood! As predicted, they march wide legged to the locker room. Hunter leads the pack. Grunts, moans and groans hover in the shower stalls. After the group cleans up, they disband until their next session. Each vowing not to expose infidelities of the other.

(Canine Encounter)

Not driving to the gym today, Hunter takes a leisurely jog home to maintain his cardio heart rate. While meandering on foot through the city, he startles a massive Doberman Pinscher as he rummages through trash. Feeling threatened by Hunter's proximity, the Doberman's ears perk while he begins to growl. Hunter knows not to run inciting an incident. However, his ploy failed. The Doberman gives chase to Hunter! Although Hunter is a decent sprinter, he cannot outpace the Doberman due to Hunter's bulky build. Leaping over small obstacles proves quite challenging for the mammoth behemoth. Tripping on a loosened shoe lace, Hunter tumbles to the ground. The Doberman manages to nip his calf slightly breaking Hunter's skin. Before any more damage is inflicted, Hunter swings a wooden plank lying next to him. Fortunately, the dog retreats behind a ragged fence. Hunter rises to his feet, patting the grit away from his body. He limps a bit down the sidewalk heading home just yards away.

Once at home, he peeps through the fence not seeing Sybil in the backyard. He tips inside to the downstairs bathroom. Hunter quietly closes the door as not to alert Sybil of his arrival. Looking backwards in the bathroom

mirror, hunter dabs some hydrogen peroxide on the miniscule puncture. As his wife, he too dismisses the incident not feeling in danger. After tiptoeing upstairs, he discovers Sybil sound asleep in the bed. He joins her for a much needed nap. The duo slumbers into the next morning without any recall memory of their animal events!

(Rise and Shine)

The wind rustles some debris hitting the upstairs window. Sybil immediately awakens like lightning. Paranoid she leaps to her feet hurriedly getting ready for work. Glancing at her floral wall calendar, she realizes it's a National Holiday. She sighs a relief! Hunter too awakens. He's not alarmed due to his night work as a bouncer. Sybil slinks back between the covers. The newlyweds chit chats. "So, how was your workout yesterday baby?" "As far as I remember, pretty well. You remember I am training for another show?" "Yes, sweetie. We are both in the competitive zone. I will be entering a gardening contest myself. I'm confident we'll both bring home first place!" Stroking each other's egos with gentle caresses, and tender nothings, love making progressively ensues. Hunter flips Sybil over like a pancake for some "Doggy Styled" loving!

Once the raw passion concludes, the two enjoy a glass of refreshing iced tea on the outside terrace. They prop their feet up soaking the beauty of Texas sky. Sybil draws Hunter's attention to her garden's grandeur. "Wow Sybil. You have the green thumb touch. You are gonna win hands down when you enter the contest." Sybil blushes. She leans over smooching Hunter's cheek. Their bliss is interrupted

by an eight legged visitor weaving construction. "Shit, a spider! I hate spiders!" shouts Hunter. As he rises to his feet to annihilate the arachnid, Sybil leaps into action, grabbing Hunter's wrist with supercharged reflexes! "It's a simple garden spider sweetie. Let her be. She's gonna eat pests in the garden." "Damn, I have never seen you move so fast!" replies Hunter with amazement. "Yea, I don't know what came over me snatching your wrist like that. However, please let her do her thing ok." With hesitation, Hunter agrees. After a few more hours of basking, Sybil and Hunter head inside. Hunter showers, while Sybil begins dinner plans.

(Manifestations)

Sybil decides upon an Italian dish. She gathers some tomatoes from her garden. While outside, she sees the garden spider still orbing her home. For some odd reason, Sybil extends her hand out to the arachnid as a greeting of sorts. The yellow and black web queen reciprocates. Crawling into Sybil's palm, the two make a hormonal connection! Moments later, Sybil gently places her new companion back to complete her weaving. Hunter remains upstairs grooming for work. He splashes a bit of rustic cologne across his massive chest. He selects his favorite pair of black jeans, black boots, and black tank top. Normally a neat freak, he just strews clothes on the floor like a puppy! He admires his stud reflection in the mirror. Afterwards, he saunters down the spiral staircase. He takes a whiff of kitchen aromas. "You need to toss a bit more garlic, and oregano for it to be killer casserole baby." Sybil turns around stunned, but not upset. "How can you tell that?" remarks Sybil tasting her sauce. "I can just smell it." "Wow, I didn't know you had such a sniffer." "It's a shock to me too baby." Hunter smacks Sybil's butt on the way out. He nearly forgets his manly cowboy hat.

Hunter's employer is only several blocks away so he

walks to work periodically. After clocking in, he takes his post at the door. Everyone greets him as he is an affable guy; the largest one in the bar too! It's a quiet night of beer and booze. Hunter and the other bouncer Nick, alternate door, and working the floor duties. Patrolling the parking lot for shady activity, and dispensing the occasional brew defines them. Keepers of peace; champions of the weak. The old fashioned juke box is spinning. Kenny Rogers, Dolly Parton, Johnny Cash, Loretta Lynn, Tammy Wynette and Glen Campbell are featured favorites! Laughter, merriment and dancing are galore!

(Who let the dog out?)

Good times continue until some good ole country boys arrive. Local okie dokes with mischief rampant. They are already liquored up from some local moonshine! Bubba, Billy Joe, Jesse, Earl Jr. and Jeb stumble around the bar. Their 'redneck' monkeyshines are disturbing to the patrons. The bar owner, Red, motions Nick, Hunter's co-bouncer, to escort the rowdy rednecks out. Nick was closet to them. The dominant instincts of a dog emerge! Hunter's veins begin to swell with testosterone and then some! Hunter instructs Nick to back off as Hunter is the "Alpha Male." With a slight growling noise, Hunter tosses each one out effortlessly as feathers! He rumbles in the parking lot fighting all 5 at the same time. Hunter becomes a beastly brute! He easily over powers the horde! Witnessing the brawl, Nick comes out pleading with Hunter to calm down. In a fit of senseless rage, Hunter decks Nick in the jaw!

The crowd gathers outside to video for social media upload. Red, the bar owner, throws his polishing cloth to the floor running outside halting the ruckus. He and Nick have to nearly crowbar themselves between Hunter. "Hunter, snap out of it!" The witless rednecks high tail it for their backwoods lives. "It's over! What the hell has come

over you? I have never seen you behave this way before. Go home and work it off. I'll see you tomorrow for your shift in restrained, more tamed form." Hunter snaps out of his fogginess shaking his head. "I'm sorry Red for what happened. I don't know what came over me." Hunter holds his head down with embarrassment. He also shakes Nick's hand providing an apology to his peer bruiser. Red and Nick pat him on the back as forgiveness. After grabbing his cowboy hat, Hunter begins his walk home.

(A Man and His Dog)

Still reeling from his ordeal, Hunter walks home in the Texas heat. It's dark, but the humidity lingers. His boots are reeling from perspiration. He removes hit hat wiping the sweat from his brow profusely. As karma has it, Hunter crosses paths with a familiar figure. He squints his eyes for better acuity. It's the exact stray Doberman Pinscher that bit him days before! Hunter feels a Deja vue, but can't exactly recall. The two make eye contact starring each other down as in a game of chicken. Hunter does not retreat! Instead, he growls at the dog! Submissively, the dog whimpers while sitting on its hind legs. An unspoken dominance has occurred! Under canine subjection, Hunter eases up as if mentally commanding the dog to follow him. Two canine spirits bond; one with four legs, the other with two!

Once arriving home, Hunter pets his new companion/ subordinate giving him entry in the back yard. The gate hinges are a bit rusty, so Hunter eases the gate delicately. The dog roams, sniffing his new territory. Nearly a minute later, Hunter pats his leg double time beckoning his Doberman. Hunter stoops down, and says… "Your name is Duke." Duke connects with his new master in unspoken ways. Moments later, Hunter didn't have to fumble for his

backdoor keys in the dark. His night vision has vastly been augmented! Unlocking the rear entrance, Hunter creeps in silently. He wants to surprise Sybil with the news the next day!

(Arachnid meets Canine)

The birds are chirping with melodic praises. Sybil didn't sleep soundly. She was drawn to the prior night's darkness. It's good their bedroom isn't facing the backyard. Sybil rolls over reaching for Hunter, but he's bed absent! "Ruff! Ruff, Ruff!" Duke is barking at the garden spider elevated near the gutters. Disturbed by the near proximity of barking, Sybil rushes down stairs where Hunter is preparing homemade dog food. He slept downstairs on the couch last night. "Hunter, I think there is a loose dog nearby," raves Sybil! Hunter is a bit disappointed that Duke announced his presence before he could. He takes Sybil by the hand, escorting her to the backyard. Her eyes are closed, but barking increases. "Open your eyes Sybil for a big surprise!"

Becoming nervous from barking, Sybil opens her eyes. Sybil is stricken. Her heart pounds nearly bursting her ribcage! Sybil screams in distress! "Nooooooo! I'm terrified of dogs Hunter! Get rid of it now! Trying to appease his new bride, he tells her Duke followed him home last night. Sybil is not having it. Something defensive arises in Hunter. His veins begin to swell! He snaps fiercely, as protecting a "pack" member... "I hate spiders! Your spider lives here, and so is my dog!" Duke knowingly struts around with a

victory dance after Hunter snarls at Sybil. Sybil is shook up, and storms inside! She peeps out a window disgusted by the playful pair. Still huffing, Sybil hurriedly dresses for her Librarian shift downtown. Hunter remains disconnected. He labors constructing a dog house from some old lumber in storage. He too has to work later at the bar.

(Minerva)

While at the Library, Sybil has the urge to research Spiders. She scours the web (LOL), and grabs books from shelves. She consumes data. The more she reads, the more enthralled she becomes! Several patrons waiting at the counter for assistance feel slighted and walk out! Noticing the incident, her supervisor admonishes her. "Sybil, two valued patrons just walked out due to your inattentiveness. I'm quite in shock. This is so unlike you being preoccupied. You are the best worker I employ. Please don't let this happen again." Sybil takes a deep breath nodding her head. She is too flustered to verbally comment. She gathers herself for the job duties at hand. During allotted breaks, Sybil conducts additional research. Once her shift is complete, she eagerly cranks her ancient, jalopy VW bug, and hurries home. It's fuming white smoke as an unregulated nuclear power plant!

Once arriving at home, Hunter has already departed for his shift at the bar. Sybil reheats leftover Italian. Two glasses of wine compliment the experience. Feeling liberated, Sybil unravels her flowing auburn hair. Dusk settles. Sybil feels the allure of a darkening sky, and heads outside on the patio. Much to her malcontent, Sybil sees a doghouse with its occupant. Duke growls at the female.

Sybil's fears are waning! An exotic confidence pulsates! She stands her ground! Duke slowly backs down, retreating to his dog house. He maintains a wolf's sharp focus on her. In defiance, Sybil walks to the gardens spider's web with open hand. The spider lowers herself down with her silk thread. Sybil raises her friend to her lips; kissing the spider saying… "Your name is Minerva."

(Meanwhile at the Bar)

It's another sellout crowd at Red's Grill and Bar. It's Burger Night; half off. Hunter is working the floor along with Nick maintaining civility. The smokey, Tex/Mex flavors of Red's burgers are legendary. His steak fries are equally delicious. Hunter is wolfing down those burgers on his break! Juices run down his cheek. Once a well done burger type guy, he now desires rare! Things really begin to jump when the live band perform! Their fiddle play, and rhythmic boot stomping rile the patrons. Red is shaking hands with guests making his rounds. Business is great tonight! During the midst of all the "yee-haw," Dixie saunters into the bar. She is the hottest chick under the roof! She quickly is gazed upon by salivating men, and jealous women! Nick too is taken by her glamour. Coming from the restroom, Hunter gazes up; smitten by Dixie! He finally gets a chance to really size her up out of the gym! Nick smiles hard heading over to personally seat Dixie. Hunter cock blocks him! He intimidates Nick, backing him off as to not causing attention to himself. Hunter pulls out Dixie's chair in a gentlemanly fashion.

A scrawny, wimpy, middle aged man becomes enraptured by Dixie. Due to his small build and awkward nature, he is

not the ladies' man. Desperate for attention, he nervously approaches Dixie. Dixie is not interested, but tries to be polite. He fumbles for words, being slightly intoxicated due to loneliness. He is harmless enough though. Dixie is still exercising her composure. She does not feel threatened, just slightly perturbed. Hunter observes the unwelcomed advances upon Dixie. He manages to summon self-control due to the prior occurrence losing his temper at the bar. Nonetheless, he keeps the little man on his radar! Minutes later, Ralph, Dixie's admirer, makes his move. He takes Dixie by the hand asking her to accompany him to a poetry reading held at the library. It's an innocent proposal.

(Hunter's Bombastic Blunder)

Hunter smells the scent of Ralph's testosterone building. Hunter's veins begin to course with rage. His alpha male ego supersedes his sense of rational judgment. In haste, he rushes to conclusions harshly! Huffing and growling, Hunter makes his way towards Ralph in heated pursuit! Before Ralph realizes what was coming, Hunter slams Ralph against the wall, raising him slowly with one hand! Dixie is aghast, but is taken by the cowboy stud. Everyone clears the area. Screams by horrified women are heard by Nick and Red. Nick rushes to the puny man's rescue, but is elbowed by Hunter knocking him off balance. "Red, I need your help" yells Nick! Fearing for their lives, the crowd stampedes the exit! Red was occupied in the back cooking more burgers and fries. Red is a sizable fella himself. It requires the full muscle might of both he and Nick to pry Hunter from the helpless man! Once freed, the little man runs for his life not looking behind.

The masses are simultaneously fearful with intrigue. Some of the same patrons that were present when Hunter went off previously were in attendance. Dixie stands by to witness the outcome. Red is furious! "Hunter, you nearly killed that man for no apparent reason! I just gave you a

warning recently for being cocky, yet you pull that same shit again. I could get sued, and lose my proprietor's license!" Red is shaking his head in disbelief and grief. "You leave me no choice son, you are fired. I'll mail your last check." Red gives Hunter his cowboy hat. Per Red's request, Nick walks Hunter off the premises. Hunter speaks to his former bouncer partner "I'm sorry dude. I've never seen you pop your cork as you have the last two nights. Something in you has changed. I hope you figure it out before it's too late man. If not, it's gonna cost you everything. Hunter holds his head down like a scolded dog walking nearly out of sight. Dixie jogs catching up to him.

(Doberman meets Poodle)

Hunter and Dixie stroll along the night sidewalk. They get to know each other. "Thanks for standing up for me back there, but he was ok… just a lonely guy looking for love is all. Funny, although you are big and handsome as hell, you don't seem like the hotheaded type. But, what do I know? I've been divorced 5 times. How 'bout you Hun?" Hunter fumbles for words. "I've never been married," stammers Hunter, but he's a convincing liar. Looking at Hunters huge hand, she notices a tan line on Hunters ring finger. She lifts his hand towards the streetlight inquiring. Hunter's tongue is silver. "Yea, I lost my High School class ring recently." "Well, at least you are an honest one. Most men in your profession, and gym lover remove their rings prior to getting down to business. It's refreshing to see an honest man for a change," replies Dixie feeling elated. Hunter blushes. "I've noticed you, and the other guys checking me out at the gym." Hunter blushes yet again with a boyish grin. "It's ok. I've been in pageants all my life. As a matter of fact, that's my nickname, Pageant." Hunter recalls what Sybil told him about winning a gardening contest, mentioning Pageant's name. Dixie is Sybil's primary nemesis. "Well this is my stop big fella." Hunter and Dixie are in front of

Dixie's apartment complex. Dixie hugs Hunter goodnight. However, he insists on escorting her to her door. She agrees. A warm embrace compliments the evening. Hunter tips his hat trotting home.

Once home, Hunter creeps in the back yard checking on Duke. Duke is wagging is nubby tail with glee! Knowing that Duke is probably starving, he uses the backdoor to retrieve more homemade dog food. Hunter spends some bonding time in the backyard. They both gaze at "Minerva" in her web with growling undertones!

(Once a Basement, now Sybil's darkened Lair)

Sybil is downstairs working on chemistry assignment for class. She has a makeshift lab. Beakers, test tubes, minerals, Periodic Table along with other Sci-Fi tangibles comprise the lab. In addition, there's a stack of books about Spiders Sybil checks out from the library. Taking a momentary break from the mad scientist demands, Sybil summons Minerva telepathically to come in the basement. Minerva scurries through an opening between the floorboards. As with Hunter and Duke, Sybil is delighted to see Minerva! Hearing voices in the basement, Hunter decides to investigate. He tries to creep down the basement floor, but due to Sybil's emerging "Spiderness," she feels the oncoming vibrations! Her head turns with quickness at Hunter's presence. "What da hell is going on down here? Sybil snaps, "Well, if you must know, I'm doing homework for class Hunter!" Hunter is taken by Sybil's sharp tone. Why are you dressed in black and stiletto heels in a basement?" "Cause I feel like it, that's why!" "How can you see to read, you barely have any light down here? Where are your eye glasses?" "I don't need them anymore, I can see well in all types of light now."

Hunter's night vision has increased to near infrared ranges. He notices the Spider inside.

"What the fuck is that Spider doing in here? I told you I hate spiders! I just saw it a few minutes ago outside." "I hate dogs!" "Her name is Minerva for future reference! As you said, your dog stays and so does my Spider!" Hunter storms off heading back upstairs from the basement. Hunter growls under his breath hating the spider invaded his turf! Angry, he goes back outside to connect with Duke for a few minutes prior to sleeping on the couch. Although Sybil is becoming like a Spider craving darkness, her human side needs sleep. Her shift at the library is approaching. Sybil grabs a spider nap upstairs bypassing Hunter snoring on the couch.

(The Pendulum Swings)

Sybil's supervisor at the Library phones her. She needs for Sybil to pull a double shift due to an employee's car accident. Sybil replies, "That's her tough luck." Not believing Sybil would say such a thing, her supervisor responds, "What did you say Sybil, must be a bad connection?" "Nothing. I'll be in shortly," remarks Sybil restraining her spider's biting wit! Sybil quickly showers. She eats some of the remaining Italian dish, while bagging the remaining portion for her lunch. She leaves Hunter to fend for himself, and his miserable dog! Hunter's acute sense of smell awakens him seconds later after Sybil whizzes by. She is having difficulty starting her worn out Volkswagen. Finally after several efforts, it starts with a backfire! Duke is stirred, and begins to bark. Hunter was peeping out the window at Sybil's distress. He didn't lift a finger to help. Instead, he headed in the backyard to comfort Duke.

Hunter decides to take Duke to the local pet store fitting him with a spiked collar, and purchasing several bags of gourmet food with other dog essentials. After done with shopping, Hunter and Duke romp around in the park for a few hours. Since Hunter has been fired, he has spare time. Heading home afterwards, Hunter notices a small

building for sale. He conceives a brilliant idea! Speeding home, Hunter phones the number of the building's for sale sign. It's somewhat dilapidated, but dirt cheap. The owner has died leaving his widow to manage the property. She eagerly accepts Hunter's offer ridding her ownership responsibilities. Fortunately, Hunter was able to file paperwork with the city all the same day. The building is his! He keeps it a secret from Sybil. While Sybil is working her library shift, Hunter and Duke inspect the premises.

(The Spider Reacts)

Instead of wearing her smock, Sybil dresses in all black. She is not appearing frumpish. Due to the Book Fair at the Library, Sybil, with the skeleton crew are rushed off their feet! Sybil tries to steal away, but she is watched like a hawk because of her recent lack of attentiveness. Children are mischievous. Being shorthanded, unfortunately, Sybil is unable to take her scheduled breaks. She desperately wants to spend time on the 'web' (pun) gazing at numerous spider species from around the world. "Sybil, you have patrons waiting on you, and a question on line 2," spews the Branch Manager! Sybil's spider nature surfaces! Sybil backslaps her boss, cursing her sharply! The sting, humiliation and insubordination of Sybil are inexcusable! "Sybil, I don't know what has come over you. You were so mild mannered in the beginning, but now you have reached the point of no return. You have developed a split personality. Sybil, fool me once shame on you, fool me twice… you are fired!" Exhaling from the encounter, Sybil feels rejuvenated with remarkable prowess exuding confident independence!

On her way out the door, now unemployed, Sybil spits on the door! She is figuratively spewing venom! Once outside, she slams her rusty car door shut nearly off the

hinges! Without fail, Sybil's car is reluctant to start. She turns it over several times until it sputters. More carbon emissions stream from the 4 wheeled Chernobyl! Puttering down the freeway, Sybil views a billboard advertisement. "Top Dollar for Crochet & Needlepoint… Skilled Weavers Only." Although Sybil has never hewn a stitch with thread or otherwise, an internal drive beckons her! Taking a detour, she stops at an Art and Crafts Boutique brimming with yarns, threads, beads, glitter and other tools of the craft. Sybil departs with several bags overflowing with embroidery knick knacks. She makes a mad rush home, although her car is in slow motion!

(Awkward Appetites)

Feeling frisky as a playful canine, Hunter waits upstairs for his wife to arrive home. His instincts for sexual gratification peak as a dog in heat! Hunter and Duke had their day on the town (as it were), earlier becoming acquainted with Hunter's new building. Sybil arrives home with totes in hand full of yarns, threads, needles, etc. Sybil goes to the basement with her goody bags placing them aside for a moment. Afterwards, she goes upstairs where she finds Hunter nude, "lubed up" for intercourse. She just dismisses him while seated at her bathroom vanity. She begins to brush her flowing hair. It has darkened, becoming fuller bodied, thickened with volume since her spider bite. Hunter stands in front of the master bathroom entrance. He strokes his cock trying to entice Sybil. She smirks at his pretense. "If you fuck me, then I will have to kill you afterwards." (Spiders in the wild have a tendency to kill/cannibalize the males after mating.) "So if I were you, I suggest that you go fuck yourself."

Hunter is deflated. He growls a bit then whimpers due to rejection. His cock goes from "Stud" to "Dud!" Sybil chuckles. Moments later, she retreats to her darkened basement to begin her Knitting/Crocheting. Although Sybil

has never completed a stitch, her new spiderlike abilities enable her to knit with lightning speed and exquisite, artful design. Once only right handed, now Sybil has the dexterity of being ambidextrous! Sybil telepathically summons Minerva to join her by her side. Minerva serves as inspiration and welcomed company. Sybil plans on supporting herself solely upon her winnings from the knitting/crocheting contests. Sybil and Hunter become more isolated as their animal tendencies surface.

(Webs and Doghouses)

Both Hunter and Sybil do not share what happened with their jobs. Each feign as their workday charade cloaking their true motives! Hunter uses his saving to remodel his building into his own personal haven for likeminded men! It's called "The Dog Pound." There's a lot of whimsical doggy décor. The entrance archway is shaped like a doghouse entrance. There are several fire hydrants, dog tags, leashes, and edible goodies shaped like bones, etc. After several weeks of refurbishments, it's opening night. It's a full sized club with seating. It's an exclusive men's club only. Cigarettes, cigars, gambling and booze are permitted. Pornography with X Rated Films are viewed on the 60 inch flat screen. Hunter elicits the assistance of his gym buddies to help staff/man the club. The fellas comply. Hunter pays them under the table. Hunter even converts a portion of the club into a fully functioning gym! As word spreads about the "Dog Pound," business booms. Duke even has his own doggy pad at the club.

Sybil loses herself in her gardening, chemistry courses and her ever growing allure for spiders. As a spider sheds, so has Sybil's mundane, meek, introverted demeanor and wardrobe. Being already intellectual, the spider bite adds

to her aptitude. She is acing every course. Inherently, her garden flourishes in majestic manner. Minerva is devouring harmful garden/flora insects. She too is enterprising with profitable income. Sybil's exquisite flair for intricate, meticulous, and highly imaginative needle point creations net her continuous, tidy profits. Her spider blood grants her unrivaled domination against all competitors! She is setting her sights on crushing the garden expo!

(Spider Repelling and Dog Taming)

Hunter's abhorrent detest of spiders, and Sybil's hatred of dogs increases exponentially. Sybil is finding it quite difficult to till her garden due to the evil eyes of Duke. Duke becomes especially peeved when Minerva, Sybil's spider cohort, is near. At times, Duke nearly foams at the mouth! He wants so terribly to chomp both Sybil and Minerva. Sybil stands her ground while shielding Minerva from Duke's hostilities. Sybil's garden is thriving with blooming blossoms, accompanied by a cornucopia of vegetable goodies! Mother Nature is on her side, nonetheless; Duke is a thorn in her side! While extracting weeds in her brimmed hat and shades, Sybil recalls an old "Tom and Jerry" cartoon episode from early childhood. Tom stumbles upon an ultrasonic dog whistle that keeps Butch, his dog nemesis, at bay. The ultrasonic whistle when blown caused excruciating, paralyzing audio pain for dogs, used for obedience training, but was harmless to humans. Sybil grins at Duke while giving him the middle finger! Sybil arrives at a stopping point then heads to the pet store buying her secret weapon!

Hunter is getting tired of Sybil's "buddy-buddy" relationship with Minerva. Sybil and He are barely on

speaking terms. He's pissed off at the black and yellow carnivore! Hunter sees Minerva in the house more frequently scurrying around baseboards. Previously, He and Sybil had a near drag out confrontation about Duke becoming a house dog. During the argument, Sybil stood on her tip toes, abrasively defying Hunter's request! She told him he would have hell to pay if Duke crossed the threshold, and she meant that shit! Possessing a wolf's sly cunning for instincts, Hunter smirks at Sybil; biding his time. Before going to his club, Hunter stops to the Home and Hardware store. He canvasses the aisles reading bug spray labels. He purchases a streaming can of "Spider Kill" guaranteed to send any spider belly up, legs curled from 20 feet away!

(Vroom! Vroom!)

Both Sybil and Hunter are scoring major cash with their ventures. Hunter decides to spike his game purchasing a classic Harley Davidson motorcycle. It's deafening, shiny, heavy, and beefy with leather accents. Hunter transacts with the bike shop for some customized modifications. Of course, he incorporates dog/canine artwork throughout the design process. He even has a rear trailer car and hitch for Duke to ride in! When weather permits, he opts for his bike versus his 4 wheeled automobile. Sybil hates the brutish machine, but she counters!

Feeling more exotic and liberated by the moment, Sybil has reached her boiling point with her rust bucket car! Enough is enough! While car shopping online, she discovers the object of her desire. It's a jet black, 2 doors, turbo charged, 6 speed manual Nissan 300 Z Convertible. It's in mint condition for sale buy a local owner. Coincidentally, it's the same woman who sold the building to Hunter! She is still liquidating some of her late husband's assets. Like Hunter's acquisition, Sybil shrewdly makes out like a bandit! Hunter snubs Sybil's "Spider-like" vehicle. Obsessed with her arachnid within, Sybil gets her ride customized too! An auto shop specializing in graphic paint designs, masterfully

crafts a huge Garden Spider on both rear fender panels. Weeks later, she receives a personalized license plate from DMV saying "SPDRWOMN." Sybil gets her rocks off by driving the interstate at full throttle speeds, top down, around 2am nightly, with turbulent winds whipping her now all black hair! As most spiders, she's transforming nocturnal. Her night vision is so evolved; she wears shades driving in complete darkness!

(Some Trot Others Crawl)

Hunter becomes quite the entrepreneur. Murmurings of his exclusive "Dog Pound Club," permeate the underground. Biker gangs, Veterans, muscle boys, bears, chubs, daddies, and countless blue collar workers patronize Hunter's club. Hunter's dog, Duke, becomes the mascot! No other club around has smoking with alcoholic beverages, and also now featuring an environmentally health conscious gym under one roof! A dual revenue flow; gym memberships, and club dues. Although such an antithesis, however; the polarity oxymoron works well. Even Red and Nick pay Hunter a visit. They are impressed with Hunter's business model. Hunter holds no hard feelings, but he sticks out his chest in "Alpha Male" fashion. Between managing the club, Hunter puts his gym equipment through its paces. He's training hard to win the "Buff Bod" competition.

Sybil continues her dual pursuits. Her knitting/ crocheting/needlepoint remains her current bread and butter. A world renowned collector is paying top dollar for everything Sybil fashions. Spider blood makes it so damn easy! In her basement, makeshift lab, she concocts two secret formulas! First, an eco-friendly, organic garden pesticide that's of course harmless to any spider. Secondly,

an organic, compound elixir which naturally increases flower and vegetable growth! Unlike and yet similar in facets, Sybil is setting her sights on a blue ribbon for her gardening competition. Through the grapevine, she still hears about a woman named "Pageant" aka "Dixie," who claims first prize every entry!

(Kryptonite)

The newlyweds are becoming more estranged with each day. Opposites attract with magnets, however; not with this Adam and Eve! On one particular day, Hunter and Duke were goofing in the backyard. Duke begins barking excessively communicating merriment with his master. As a result, Sybil pounds on the window frame attempting to get Hunter to shut the dog up. Hunter turns around hearing his wife's discontent. Nonetheless, he eggs Duke on becoming more rambunctious! Fed up with the bullshit, Sybil snatches the ultrasonic dog whistle from her purse! She blows it with all her might! Consequently, she observes Duke whimpering, falling to the ground. Even more revealing, Sybil witnesses Hunter covering his ears curling up in fetal position on the grass yelling..."AWWWWWWWW, THE PAIN!" Sybil was astounded at Hunter's shared response as Duke! She blows it more testing her mental hypothesis of Hunter's canine like hearing, detesting the sound. She rapidly tucks the dog whistle back in her purse seeing Hunter. It's all making sense to her now!

Hunter reeling from the resonation of sound slowly rises to his feet. He comforts Duke with a pat. Duke heads inside his doghouse to recover. As Hunter enters the

backdoor entrance, several, harmless "Daddy Long Legs" crawl inside. After reaching on the fridge for headache tablets, Hunter sees the Daddy Long Legs on the Kitchen wall. Hunter is livid! He quickly slams opens the sink cabinet doors retrieving his "Spider Kill Spray!" Still being present, Sybil panics begging… "NOOOOOOOOO, PLEASE, I BEG YOU DON'T DO IT!" Hunter does not care. He unleashes the toxic spray, killing the Daddy Long Legs instantly. Minute mist droplets land on Sybil's arm! She begins to convulse, writhing in sheer agony! Hunter notices similar responses between the Daddy Longs Legs and Sybil's reaction. As Sybil made her discovery earlier, Hunter too reaches his conclusion!

(Crushing It)!

It's competition day! No surprise, Hunter's and Sybil's competitions fall on the same day, at the same time! It's no real loss though since they have been at each other's throats since they were both bitten. Hunter is upstairs shaving any trace of body hair other than his head. Sybil is in her garden plucking her prized veggies and flowers. Minerva keeps her company. Duke peeps from his dog house at Sybil with Minerva. Sybil shows Duke the shiny, golden dog whistle with an evil grin. Duke gets the gist from Sybil's vibes, keeping his distance with quietness.

Hunter beats Sybil leaving the house. She hears him throttle up his Harley Davidson. Her contempt is mounting. Hunter smokes his rear tire, and then does a wheelie to spite Sybil as he speeds off! Sybil collects her most robust veggies, and vibrant flowers. After filling her basket, she too dashes out in her Nissan 300Z, Black Convertible. She adores her turbo, stick shift!

As fate operates, Sybil's and Hunter's competition is transpiring at the identical venue; the county fairgrounds. A coliseum type stage has been erected for bodybuilding competitors. Prior to competing, each had to pass a doping/steroid blood test. All passed. Fortunately for Hunter and

still undenounced to him, his fusion of 'canine' blood is not detected. As the competition stiffens, Hunter and Nick his former co-worker are the 2 finalists! (In past competitions, Nick has always been victorious; prior to Hunter's arrival to Texas). Nick flexes, contorting trying to best his buddy. Hunter returns volley. Hunter growls with dogmatic intensity, veins so pumped, nearly pierce his skin! The crowd goes insane! Hunter is crowned the winner… "Mr. Marvelous." He takes a victory walk around the stage receiving his triumphant trophy! He's the one and only Alpha Dog!

(And The Winner Is...)

Sybil with her fellow contestants are seated behind a long booth enclosure. Farmers, Botanists, Flower Shop Personnel, Nature Enthusiasts, Agricultural Lovers and the like scrutinize the scents, textures, tastes and coloration tints/hues. With clipboards in hand, accompanied by the highest discriminatory factors, the pendulum swings. At this juncture, all have been eliminated except for Sybil and Dixie (aka Pageant). For the past several years, Dixie has swept the blue ribbons in every category! However, after eyeing Sybil's flawless entries, she is not so confident! Sybil's gardening prowess, along with her own organic growth compound, not to mention her spider abilities, is too formidable! Sybil juggernauts her way to the winner's circle! First place Blue Ribbons! The audience is hailing the new kid on the block!

Dixie is devastated! This is her first defeat ever! Trying to muster dignity through failure, Dixie bundles her items, then boxing them gently in her wicker baskets. She sobs vehemently heading to her vintage El Camino. After loading her gear in the rear, Dixie drives in a daze aimlessly.

After his hands down win, Hunter heads to his favorite steak restaurant. There he orders a beer, baked potato and

Filet Mignon… of course, he wants it cooked "blood rare!" He also orders a bloody rare cut of meat for Duke. After feasting, Hunter swings by home to pick up Duke. They both head to "The Dog Pound" for late night celebrating. Hunter's gym buddies aren't sore losers although they lost to Hunter. They cheer him while working their shift. Feeling the love, Hunter announces "Drinks on the House!"

(Dog of Deception).

Intoxicated on elated euphoria, Sybil drives unrestrained and unbridled on the darkened interstate. The convertible top is down with hard rock 'n roll blasting. Her long, silky midnight black hair is twirling within the tempest. Sybil owns the night.

Hunter struts around his club with trophy in hand. The mood is charged with capacity seating. Minutes later, Dixie aka "Pageant" wanders into the festive fellowship. She's feeling somber, still numb from her loss to Sybil. Onlookers stare at her voluptuous, buxom figure; some nearly drooling! She didn't get the nickname "Pageant" by accident. Sensing Dixie's sorrow, Duke Walks up to her trying to be playful. She reciprocates. Hunter draws closer to Dixie. Hunter embraces her, and then leads her by the hand to his secluded office. Hunter orders strict instructions that he is not to be disturbed under any circumstances! Hunter and Dixie become intimate.

After some serious rallying on the asphalt, Sybil finally arrives back at home. She snacks on cold cuts, and consumes a beer. About 10 minutes later, an eerie sensation overwhelms her. It's not the alcohol, it's something mystical. She lies across the sofa honing in. Her "Spider Sense" is

serves as precognition. She mentally receives a cloudy, psychic apparition. Sybil sees what appears to be Hunter in a compromising position! Immediately following her mental vision, she rushes to the backyard. She telepathically commands Minerva in her palm. Sybil tells Minerva to track down Hunter. Minerva scurries off in obedience.

(Damn Spider)!

As the love making intensifies between Sybil and Dixie, an unwelcomed spy crawls her way into Hunter's office. There was a corner hole where Minerva stealthily enters. So caught up in the moment, neither Hunter nor Dixie pay attention to the Spider spy. As Hunter did with Sybil weeks back, he screws Dixie "Doggy Style!" His massive, engorged, pinkish white cock nearly ruptures. The veins in his cock bulge as a tangled water hose! Just as he did with Sybil, he flips Dixie's ass over like a pancake. Dixie moans as never before spraying cum nearly across the room! She trembles in supreme ecstasy! Hunter explodes his volcano of steamy, thick, man juice on Dixie's belly! Again as with his wife, he scribbles a **"Capital H"** on Dixie's belly with his cock milk! "Dammmmmmmm.... Ahhhhhhhh.... Shiiiiiiiit...Fuck!" Hunter exclaims with his head thrown back, panting, toes curled! After regaining their composure, Hunter sees Minerva in the corner. "Damn Spider!" Hunter yells. Dixie screams! "I'm scared of Spiders!" squeals Dixie as she has a conniption! Hunter angrily grabs his boot to squash the arachnid. No cigar! Minerva's spider vision and lighting, quick reflexes prevail as she scurries back in the corner hole.

"You gotta go!" bellows Hunter as he tosses her

clothing. "I recognize that damn spider!" Dixie is jilted, heartbroken twice in a few hours! After insuring Dixie's departure out the rear deliver door, Hunter takes a shower. Luckily for him, he had equipped his club with a gym! After a quick clean, Hunter informs his staff of an emergency requiring him to leave. Hunter designates an appointee to manage in his stead until his return. Hunter grabs Duke placing him in his rear motorcycle buggy car. Hunter bolts with Duke in tow!

(Writing in the Web)

With all haste, Minerva scurries back home. She has to interpret her findings to Sybil. Her 8 legs are zooming! On a mission, Hunter flees away on his bike like a bat from Hell! Unfortunately, there was a massive car accident a few miles up the road. He revs his bike's engine several times denoting his impatience. Roadblocks halted Hunter's path for nearly 20 minutes. It's a waiting game.

Once back at the house, Minerva spins an intricate, artful web as all garden spiders do. **In the web's center, is a Capital Letter "H".** Second later, they rendezvous. Minerva crawls through the floorboard gaps in the basement. Sybil is in the basement eager and brooding. With Sybil's palm open, Minerva perches and translates what she witnessed. Sybil is raging mad when she discovers Hunter has his own business, and moreover he had sex with another woman… **squirting an "H" in Cum on her body as Hunter did with her! Hunter aka "Zorro," strikes again!**

(Reaping Time)

Hunter finally arrives home. He glances at what appears to be a **"Capital H"** <u>woven in a web outside!</u> He's momentarily stunned observing the marvel! His wolf instincts sense tension in the midst. Duke is right by Hunter's side. With his keen hearing, Hunter knows Sybil is in the basement. Hunter and Duke descend the stairwell cautiously. Its pitch black in Sybil's lair. The two exchange words in ecliptic darkness. "Can you see well enough Hunter? Is it too dark for you down here?" Hunter replies subtly… "I can see just as well as you can." Hunter has his infrared canine vision. Sybil has her nocturnal spider sight. Sybil replies… "Oh, I know. I'm sure you can. Got your partner in crime Duke with you huh?" "Yea, as you do with Minerva clinging to your shirt." Minerva told me everything," replies Sybil. "You are a lying, cheating, backstabbing, obnoxious, meat-headed, low nuts hanging, no neck, wannabe, two-legged dog motherfucker!" Still in complete darkness, Hunter verbally assaults Sybil in defense. "And you my dear are a psycho, schizophrenic, bipolar, nutty as a fruitcake, bloodsucking, Elvira, Goth, spider freak bitch!"

(Straight to the Jugular)

Hostilities become physical madness! Sybil and Hunter unleash! Both command their animals to attack! Duke begins to maul Sybil with ferocity! Blood gushes from open wounds! Minerva leaps onto Hunter biting him violently several times on all exposed skin! Her fangs pierce like sewing needles! Both in agony, Hunter reaches in his back pocket pulling out the can of "Spider Kill"! He frantically saturates Minerva and Sybil! Possessing her own equalizer, Sybil blows hard on the ultrasonic dog whistle! Hunter yells out in pain! Duke cries like a scalded dog! Their eardrums burst, while causing a fatal aneurism! Sybil and Minerva writhe, and contort from the "Spider Kill!" It feels like burning acid of death! Moments pass, the quad are motionless on the cold basement floor.

City Detectives discover the dead bodies of Hunter and Sybil. They are baffled at the macabre, morbid scene. "Looks like a case of simple domestic violence," a rookie stated. Upon closer inspection of the scene, Grace, a veteran detective notes it was something more sinister. The emptied can of Spider Kill, and the ultrasonic dog whistle are gathered as evidence. Duke and Minerva are dead, clamped on the jugulars of their intended victims! After reaching a hypothesis, Grace rises to her feet after kneeling from taking photos.

Grace makes a chilling assessment...

"Men Are *Dangerous* Dogs." 'Women Are *Devious* Spiders."